TINSEL & TUSKS

LOVE AT FIRST ORC, BOOK 3

AVA ROSS

ENCHANTED STAR PRESS

TINSEL & TUSKS

Love at First Orc, Book 3

Copyright © 2023 Ava Ross

All rights reserved.

No part of this book may be reproduced in any form or by any electronic or mechanical means, including information storage and retrieval systems, without written permission from the author, except for the use of brief quotations with prior approval. Names, characters, events, and incidents are a product of the author's imagination. Any resemblance to an actual person, living or dead, is entirely coincidental.

Cover art by Wolfraven Studio

Editing/Proofreading by JA Wren & Owl Eyes Proofs & Edits

*For my parents & family who
always believed I could do this.*

TINSEL & TUSKS

I'm snowbound with a gorgeous orc businessman. Will sharing the holiday season melt his grumpy heart?

When the blizzard of the century hits my small New England town, I'm stuck spending Christmas in my tiny home with only Milo, my mischievous pup. My kitchen's full of cookie dough in need of baking, and my holiday cheer is melting faster than the mini marshmallows in my mug of hot cocoa. Until Milo leads me on an icy slide down the driveway and straight into the arms of Vestalon—a gorgeous orc businessman who crashed his truck into a tree.

I offer him shelter from the storm, and soon, we're snowbound together. As the fire crackles, Milo plays matchmaker, ensuring heated moments with Vestalon beneath the mistletoe and an unexpected surprise in the shower.

But when the snowflakes settle and the storm subsides, will Vestalon return to his bustling city job, or will he choose to stay in this winter wonderland with me and Milo?

Tinsel & Tusks is set in the Love At First Orc Series. Expect to be snowed in with a billionaire orc businessman who's creative with his . . . (cough), size difference, only one bed/forced proximity, a matchmaking pup, a shy, curvy woman in need of love, fated mates in heat, and plenty of holiday fun. HEA guaranteed.

Love at First Orc Series
Orc Charming
(Free with Newsletter Sign-up)

Orc-us Pocus
Orc-ishly Ever After
Tinsel & Tusks
Orc-wardly Yours
Gaming the Orc

Single Orc Dad
(Also part of the Sweet Monster Treats shared world)

CHAPTER 1
EMMA

The faint smell of pine needles drifted through the air as I sat on my sofa dressed in my one-piece fox PJs with matching fox slippers. I even had a fluffy fox tail.

They were silly things, but if there was anything I'd learned in my twenty-eight years of life, it was that I needed to find joy in everything I did.

My fox outfit made me happy, and that was all that mattered. At least my ex was no longer around to tell me to *change out of that stupid thing now*, and harp on me until I did it.

The sun had set, and soon, I'd have to think about making dinner—alone. I should be happy about that, right? I loved that I could make what *I* wanted, *when* I wanted it, rather than having to cater to someone else's needs.

I lifted my mug of hot cocoa off the coffee table and took a sip, staring into the flames crackling merrily in the fireplace. Christmas music played on the TV, and if I got a bit teary when the woman sang about being home for Christmas to be with someone she loved, that was okay too. I didn't need a guy to make me feel complete. I was proud of my job at the local library, my cozy one-bedroom home that I owned all by myself, and the new life I'd begun in this New England town.

Milo, my black-furred mutt, twitched on the sofa beside me, chasing doggie ghosts through the snow. When I patted him, his bushy tail flopped around and he settled, sliding into sugarplum dreams. Or, in his case, dreams of big bones and endless tennis balls flying through the air.

I wouldn't be traveling to spend my vacation holiday week with family. The cost of plane tickets was too much for my small budget, and if I was being honest, we weren't that close anyway. All I needed was Milo.

Mostly.

I'd been divorced for a year, and lately, I'd begun to wonder what it would be like to share my life with someone special. Did I dare trust my heart with a new guy?

I wasn't sure.

With a sigh, I glanced around my living room. The cutest Christmas tree ever stood proudly in the corner, decorated with colorful ornaments and twinkling lights. I'd even picked up some orc ornaments in town because who didn't want orcs dangling on their tree?

A few years ago, orcs emerged from a mountain range in the middle of the country and joined human society.

They took jobs and even dated us. *Us* being figurative. I hadn't dated an orc—yet—though I was intrigued by the idea.

I'd cut the Charlie Brown tree this morning and dragged it across the back field and inside my tiny home. If some of the needles had fallen off and it was a bit too bare on one side, who cared? I loved it because it was imperfect, just like me.

Milo stirred again, but this time, pats didn't soothe him. He leaped off the sofa and his claws tap-tap-tapped across the old wooden floorboards as he left the living room, scooting into the front hall, where he barked.

"No, please," I groaned, though I sent him a rueful smile. "Pretty please, buddy? You just went out."

He punctuated his bark with a whine.

"Okay, okay. I'm coming," I sighed, setting my mug down and making my way to the entrance, my fox slippers swishing on the floor. "When you've gotta go, you gotta go, right?"

Milo's unbent ear quirked my way, and his bushy tail flipped around.

"You know it's snowing outside," I said, grabbing his leash off the hook.

He yipped and scratched at the door.

"Okay, but this is it. The last thing we need to do is get up in the middle of the night because you didn't finish." I shook my finger at him. "No sniffing all the bushes this time. And I'm telling you right now, you're not going to find that tennis ball you left outside weeks ago, so no looking. Got it?"

He gave me a doggy grin, and his tail wagged faster.

I dragged on my winter coat and gloves and clipped Milo to his leash. When I opened the door, the entire blizzard (or what felt like it) blasted inside with a frigid gust of air.

"Ugh. Can't you use the pee pad?" I asked.

Milo charged outside, dragging me along with him before I could contemplate putting on my boots.

Well, he wouldn't stay out long in a storm, so foxy feet it is.

Instead of doing his business along the side of the walk, Milo darted out onto the driveway, tugging me behind him.

"Milo, buddy, what's gotten into you?" I called out, nearly losing my footing on the slippery ground.

Milo led me on the equivalent of a sled ride down the driveway that ended at the winding country road. Snow pelted my face, and the wind threatened to rip off my coat.

Lights bloomed ahead, and if they'd kept moving, I would've waved and made Milo return to the house pronto.

But the lights didn't move. And when I squinted through the falling snowflakes, it appeared as if the lights were pointing toward the woods along one side of my driveway. That didn't make sense.

As Milo hauled me closer, I gasped. A black truck the size orcs used since human-sized cars were a tight fit, had left the road and slid across the end of my driveway, crashing into a big old oak tree. The headlights stabbed toward the forest, and from where I held Milo back, it appeared no one was moving inside the cab.

Milo whined and looked from me to the truck, his gaze full of worry.

With adrenaline surging through my veins, I hurried over to the driver's side door and grabbed the mirror, using it to step up onto the running board. My eyes widened when I peered inside.

An orc male dressed in an immaculate black business suit lay slumped across the steering wheel, unmoving. A bluish bruise was already forming on his forehead where it must've impacted with the windshield.

"Hey," I called out, then louder. "Hey! Are you okay in there?"

The orc didn't stir. He must be unconscious.

Oh shit, what if he was dead?

And why hadn't I brought my phone? Then I could've called 9-1-1, waited for them to arrive, and made sure he'd be alright.

"Should I return to the house and make the call?" I asked the world in general.

Milo yipped, and I swore he shook his head. Sometimes, this dog surprised me with how uncanny he was.

"You're saying I need to take care of this myself," I said, and Milo barked again in affirmation.

Alrighty. I hopped back to the ground and wrenched on the door handle; grateful it was unlocked.

I climbed into the truck, sucking in the lingering warmth inside the cab. "Hey, are you okay? Can you hear me?"

The orc shifted, groaning. Thankfully, he wasn't dead. He flopped back against the seat and his head lolled, his eyes remaining shut.

"I'm going to help you." How in the world I was going to do something like that? I wasn't superwoman, capable of lifting ginormous orcs with one hand.

I unbuckled his seatbelt and shook his shoulders. "Hey, orc dude. I need you to wake up."

He huffed and his eyes opened, his gorgeous golden gaze meeting mine.

Let me amend that to *sexy* orc dude.

Before I could try to rouse him further, he tumbled out of the vehicle, knocking us both to the ground in the snowbank piling up beside his truck.

The big burly orc landed on top of me, pinning me to the ground.

Of course.

CHAPTER 2
VESTALON

Something infernally shrill was yipping nearby, and I lay on top of a woman while something cold nipped at my neck.

My head throbbed like a thousand orcs were stomping through it.

Where was I and how had I gotten here?

Headache.

Female lying beneath me.

Had I gotten drunk and gone home with someone? That would be a first for me, but I'd recently decided I needed to let loose every now and then. I could've . . . let loose. Somehow.

Lifting my head, I peered down at the woman, taking in her medium toned skin and her nose dotted with cute freckles. Her hair spread out from her face in a light brown fan, and she had the prettiest green eyes I'd ever seen.

I approved of my drunk taste.

"You're awake," she cried, clutching my shoulders.

"Yes, I am."

She wore a winter coat—an odd choice for bed sport —and what appeared to be a . . . fox suit beneath. I had to be mistaken about the latter. If we'd hooked up last night, she'd be naked, right?

Although, if I passed out before . . . doing whatever I might've planned, she could still be dressed.

"We appear to be wearing too much clothing," I said. "Give me a moment to clear my head, and I'll rectify that." I frowned. "Why is it so cold here? Do you have a window open, woman?"

"Let me up!"

My gaze homed in on her mouth. Such plump, ripe lips in a ruby shade I adored. Maybe before stripping, I'd have a taste . . .

I captured her mouth and groaned on connection. Heat flared across my skin, threatening to burn me alive.

She smacked my shoulder and while her mouth softened, I sensed she wasn't as excited about this as me.

Something was licking my right ankle, distracting me from her wonderful scent and taste.

I lifted my head.

"Get off me, you, you . . . you brute." she said with a glare. She bucked, and I rolled to the side, landing on my back on an incredibly cold surface. At least whatever was licking my ankle stopped.

Snow?

It swirled around us, coated us.

"We're not in your bedroom," I said.

"Great observation."

A small black dog scampered up beside my head and licked my face until I nudged it away. It sat, its black fluffy tail stirring up the snow behind it.

"I'm *not* drunk," I muttered.

"I certainly hope not," she said, clearly perturbed. "You were driving."

"We're *not* in bed together, eager to have sex."

"Your kiss wasn't *that* good."

I huffed. "My kisses are amazing."

"Not when I'm lying in a snowbank in the middle of a blizzard."

Sitting up, I clutched my head. When it stopped spinning, I peered around, taking in my truck impaling a large tree and the snowy world around me. "I remember now. I got lost on my way to Settler's Cove."

"That's one town over." She also sat.

My frown deepened. "Why are you wearing a fox suit?"

"Because I like it. It makes me smile, and I'm all about feeling happy."

I stared at her fox clad feet with bushy tails on the heels. "I see." Truly, I didn't.

"Are you okay?" she asked, her face knitting with concern.

"I believe so."

Seeing her sympathy made my insides knot tight. It was a good and not so good feeling because . . . I shook my head.

No. She was not my fated mate.

Then I remembered our very brief kiss and my response to it.

It couldn't be.

"My truck appears to be trying to wrap itself around a tree," I said to distract myself from that train of thought. "I remember losing control in the snow, sliding off the road."

"You hit your head on the windshield." She pointed to my left temple where my head throbbed the most. "You should go to the ER and get it checked out."

"I'm fine."

Rising to her feet, she shrugged. "It's up to you. If you've got a subdural hematoma and you don't want your brain . . . evacuated, or whatever they do, that's also your choice."

I also got up, and I hated that I swayed and she had to grab my arm to steady me. Pulling my phone from my pocket, I swiped into it and scowled. "No service. Do you have a landline?"

"Why would I?" She picked up the small dog who wiggled and licked her chin.

"Some rural communities require it for internet."

"Mine doesn't. We're not that backwoods here."

That was a matter of perception.

"Come up to my house," she gestured to the snow-covered driveway. "My cell phone should have service."

"You didn't bring it with you."

"Why would I? I only took Milo outside to go pee. He led me on a wild chase down my driveway, and I guess it's a good thing that he did, because I found you slumped across your steering wheel. You could've frozen to death."

"I appreciate your assistance. I'm Vestalon Noalrid, by the way."

She gave me a nod. "Emma Wright. Let's get you inside before we both freeze to death." Shivers took over her frame, and she clung to her pup. Oddly enough, I wanted her to cling to me just as tightly.

I shook off the feeling.

"Sure," I said. "And thank you."

"For what?"

"Rescuing me."

"Oh, you're welcome. You'd do the same."

As I followed her up the driveway, I suspected Emma had rescued me from more than just the accident.

CHAPTER 3
EMMA

"A good kisser, huh?" I huffed to myself as I approached the front of my tidy home. "That's a matter of perspective."

Lights gleamed in the living room, and it looked so cozy from out in the frigid storm, I almost wanted to cry. "It was an alright kiss," I muttered. "Forced, which is never fun."

"I didn't exactly force you to kiss me," Vestalon said gruffly from beside me.

"What do you call it, then?"

"A spontaneous thing?"

"It *was* spontaneous. I'll give you that." Who kissed a woman for the first time they met them and while lying in a snowbank? Vestalon, obviously.

"I apologize. I thought . . ."

"You thought I was your plaything and that we were in bed together." I rolled my eyes. He was just like my ex, who'd cheated on me almost from the moment we got married—and probably *before* we'd said I do. "I don't know how you live, but I don't lie around in the snow making out with strange guys."

He sent me a lopsided grin. "Maybe you should."

I huffed again and took the steps to my front porch, leading him inside. After putting Milo down on the floor and removing his leash and harness, I wrangled out of my coat, hanging it on a peg.

I ditched my slippers on the rug. My poor toes were frozen, but I slipped them into thick socks I'd left on the entryway chair, and they'd warm up quickly.

Vestalon heeled off his dress shoes and removed his business jacket, hanging it beside my coat. They looked cozy together.

"No more kisses," I declared.

"Not unless you ask." He stood in his black stockings, peering around. "Quaint."

"Why does that word always sound insulting?"

His brow ridge lifted. "I wasn't trying to insult you."

When he rolled up his white dress shirt sleeves, I tried not to swoon. Strong forearms were such a turn-on, especially when they were paired with incredibly wide shoulders, a narrow waist, and tree trunk thighs that stretched the fabric of his black pants. He unbuttoned the top of his shirt, exposing orc-green skin that was universal to his species. And why was I eager to tug his black hair out of his man bun and let it fly free?

His golden eyes were doing their own inspection of me. What did he see?

My too lush hips. Long light brown hair I usually

wore in a braid. Green eyes. The tiny dimple in my chin I felt was my best feature.

I wasn't what anyone would call beautiful, but I liked myself too much to deride the body I'd been given. It cut down my Christmas tree and hauled it inside with ease, and when I felt like it (which I almost never did), it had enough oomph to go for a run.

He probably noticed I was a lot shorter than him. If we embraced, my mouth would be at about the right height to suck on his nipples.

Ugh. I needed to stop thinking about this guy and sex.

I should go into town and hit the bars, though that was totally not my thing. But I must have an itch that needed scratching.

"Phone?" he asked, his gruff voice startling me out of my ongoing perusal of his delectable shape.

"It's in the living room."

He followed me, stopping inside the double arched doorway, his appreciative gaze taking in the fire that needed feeding, my couch with colorful pillows, and my lovely tree. His lips twitched. "Are those orcs ornaments?"

"Fun, right? I picked them up at the dollar store."

"You like orcs."

"Doesn't everyone?" I said breezily.

"Some."

I'd seen more prejudice against orcs than I liked, and I was vocal about knocking it down.

I lifted my phone off the coffee table and scrolled into it. "No service."

"Would you type your number into my phone?" He offered it to me.

"Why?"

"You've done a big favor for me. I could send you flowers or something to thank you, but I'd need your address. I'll text you in a day or two."

There was no harm in that. I typed it in and handed his phone back. My gaze shot to the window. "It's still snowing hard. I'm not sure we'll have service until the storm's over."

"The forecast said this is a northeaster, that it'll continue for days."

"Why were you driving during a blizzard?" The words came out like an accusation, but truly, who'd go out at a time like this unless they had to?

"My grandmother invited me to dinner, and I never say no."

That was sweet. "Where does she live?"

He named the town next up the coast from mine. "I was returning to the city, hoping to get there before it got bad, but I took a wrong turn and ended up on your road."

"It does eventually return to the main route, so you weren't far off the track. You took the scenic route."

"I didn't see much scenery."

"Because it's snowing. I mean, really. Did you—" When I caught the sparkle in his eyes, my laugh came out instead of the rest of my question. "You have a very dry sense of humor."

"Most miss it."

Yet I hadn't as far as I knew.

"My truck's off the road, so it won't cause another accident." He went to the window and peered out. "I don't believe it would be wise for me to sleep in my truck."

"I could try to take you to town."

"Do you have four-wheel-drive? Your driveway's snowed in."

"I have an SUV." But even that probably couldn't tackle this much snow.

"I could . . . wait it out on your porch."

"You'll freeze to death."

He shrugged. "I don't want to inconvenience you by . . . remaining here."

"You're suggesting hanging out with me until the storm's over?" My skin peppered with tingles, and I stepped closer to the fire, adding a few logs to keep it blazing merrily.

"Do you have a tractor I can use to pull my truck away from the tree?"

"Even if I did, I doubt your truck would run. You practically wrapped it around that poor tree."

"I'll apologize to the tree once the storm's over."

"My point is," I said, "it's going to need major work. All I've got is a push lawn mower, and I doubt that'll be of any help."

"Who plows your driveway?"

"My neighbor sometimes stops by if the snow's deep. Otherwise, I've got a snowblower."

"You do it yourself?" He appeared skeptical that I had the skill or ability to run it.

"I'm an independent woman." I lifted my chin. "I blow out my own driveway."

"Why does that sound dirty?"

I drew myself up primly, ignoring how much I was enjoying our banter. "Excuse me?"

"If someone plowed your driveway, my thought was they'd come by partway through the storm to keep it clear."

He's right. Plowing my drive did sound dirty.

"I'm afraid it'll be me and my snowblower once the storm is over."

"Yes, right. A plow truck might also be able to give me a ride into town where I could find someone to tow my vehicle into town for repairs. I could return to the city after making those arrangements."

"The garage is closed through New Year's. For Christmas."

"Orcs don't celebrate Christmas."

"Our mechanic does."

"Is he an orc?"

"Yes."

"Then he should be able to fix my truck."

"Eventually." I sunk down onto the couch and put my feet onto the table, letting them toast in the warmth from the fire. "You can stay here until the storm's over as long as you're not a serial killer."

"Would I tell you if I was?"

"Probably not. You should know that I can do taekwondo, and I'm not afraid to use it." I made fists, but truly, my only martial arts knowledge came from movies.

"I'm not a serial killer." He pressed his fist against his chest. "I appreciate your offer, and I'll take you up on it. I'll even . . ." His lips twitched upward in a devastating smile. "Blow your drive if you want."

CHAPTER 4
VESTALON

"I do my own blowing," Emma said firmly, and I could tell she was trying not to smile.

"If you insist."

Emma was the first human female I was attracted to. All the others held appeal but not enough to distract me from my work. Emma would even draw my attention if she tiptoed through my boardroom while I was chairing a vital meeting.

I settled on the couch beside her and gestured to her mug. "What are you drinking?"

"Hot cocoa, though I imagine it's cold cocoa now. Would you like some?"

I frowned at the mug. "I've never had it before. Does it taste good?"

"Why would I drink it if it didn't?" She didn't sound hostile; more amused if the quiver of her lips was anything to go by.

She was highly appealing from her lush frame to her

sharp wit. She was small compared to me. I could pick her up and plunk her on my shoulder and carry her around while barely noticing she was there.

Would she cling to my horns if I did something like that?

"I'd like some cocoa," I said gravely. "If it's not too much of a bother."

"It isn't." She rose, took her mug, and walked from the room.

I followed, unwilling to let her out of my sight. I told myself I was feeling protective, that something vicious might attack her, but other than the little black dog who scooted along with us, his tail swirling through the air, there were no beasts about.

Where was a good beast when you needed one to prove you could protect your mate?

I came to a screeching halt in the middle of her dining room while she continued to the attached kitchen. My libido kept going, telling me to check out her ripe ass, to touch it if I dared.

I'd never done something like that with anyone. It was disrespectful. But I kept getting dirty thoughts about Emma.

Hold on. What had I just thought?

Mate?

It wasn't possible.

My half-brother had mated with a human, one of his fellow teachers at the high school. Autumn was sweet, and she adored Thraal. She was kind to me, too, which I liked.

He told me she'd sparked his mating drive almost from the moment they first met.

"No," I shouted.

Emma turned back, frowning. "Are you alright?" She came back to stand in front of me and handed me her mug, which I dutifully took and placed on the dining room table. Leaping up, she quickly ran her fingertips across my forehead. "Does your head hurt? Do you feel dizzy or . . . confused?"

"I'm perfectly fine."

Except I wasn't.

"I have to get out of here," I snarled.

"We already went through that. It's storming out. Your truck's out of commission," she said. "I think you should sit down."

"No, I need to leave. Otherwise, I'm going to demand lots of sex from you."

"Um . . ." Her eyes widened.

"It's either that or I'll have to return to the orc kingdom and ride it out in a barren cave."

"Aw," she said with a sigh, leading me to one of the dining room chairs that was much too small for an orc butt. When she tugged on my shirt, I obligingly sat, perching on the edge. "Let me get you a cool cloth. We should probably try to get you to the ER in my SUV despite the deep snowbanks."

"I don't need the ER. My head's fine." I latched onto her arms, though gently. Spreading my legs, I tugged her between them, and she cooperated even in this. Her attention appeared to be fixated on my mouth.

With me sitting, we were about at eye level.

"You are my mate," I declared earnestly.

Her frown deepened. "I'm not sure I understand what you're saying. Are you sure you're not confused from a head injury?"

"You probably haven't heard of orcs going into heat."

"I'm a librarian. I read all sorts of things while I wait to help those who come in for books. I've read and heard quite a bit about orcs. While I've only met a few so far, I do know about mating and heat, but . . ." She shook her head and her expression cleared. The pretty smile that filled her face stunned me. "You're teasing me, right?"

"No tease in my words, though I find myself strangely compelled to tease your body with my tongue."

Why was I saying things like this?

Oh, I knew. I *knew*. The notion was sinking deeply into my soul.

"I'm a businessman," I insisted, overriding my mouth. "I don't use my tongue for anything outside of eating and speaking."

"Maybe you should."

A growl ripped from my chest. "Now you're the one who's teasing."

"Maybe explain what you're trying to say to me. Lay it out plainly for me."

"You, Emma, have triggered my mating heat."

CHAPTER 5
EMMA

While I wanted to remain where I was, I back out from between his nicely thick thighs.

"You did not just tell me we're mated," I barked. I put aside the "heat" part of his statement for now. Mating sounded too much like being married, and I knew where that went.

Milo yipped at my tone of voice, though his tail kept wagging. He looked from me to Vestalon as if this orc and I were best friends and about to throw a bunch of sticks for him to retrieve.

"I said mated because we are," Vestalon insisted.

"Unmate us."

"I'm afraid that's not possible." He sighed. "We'll figure something out."

"We're trapped here together for days. From what I read; close contact will deepen the bond."

"Sexual activities will deepen it further."

"Yeah, that's not going to happen."

He looked from where my hand clung to his thigh to my face, one side of his brow ridge lifting.

I snatched my hand back, clutching it to my chest. "But we don't even know each other."

"We don't need to." He rose, towering over me. "It's common for the couple to meet and know they're fated to be together immediately. They give into the heat immediately."

"So . . . So . . ." I didn't know what to say. "What am I supposed to do about this? I'm divorced, and he was a jerk. I don't want to go there again."

His snarl rumbled around us, and he glared as if my ex might be lurking underneath the dining room table. "What did he do to you? I'll rip him apart."

"While I appreciate the sentiment, he's on the other side of the country with his new wife. I'm just grateful *I'm* no longer that wife." My head tilted. "I don't know much more about orc mating customs. If I were an orc female going along with this, what would we do next?"

"I'd lift you and lay you over my shoulder, then run into the woods where I would've prepared a nest. I'd shred your clothing with my tusks and claim you."

My breath caught and my core throbbed. I ignored my body shouting out its need. "You just met me. How would you know to have a nest ready?"

"I'm speaking hypothetically here."

"Right."

"If you're satisfied, and I will make it clear right now, *you would be,* we'd be the equivalent of married when I finally released you from my nest."

"Self-confident much?" I said wryly.

He scowled. "What does that mean?"

I smirked. "All that growling that I'll be satisfied, as if it's a done deal. You need to know right now that I'm not easily satisfied, though, honestly, my only experience is with my ex, and I doubt he even tried. He was more interested in his own pleasure than mine."

"I would be focused solely on you. Believe me, you'd shriek out your joy. You'd come a million times."

I lifted one eyebrow. "A million?"

"Hypothetically."

"This assumes we'd do something like that, which we won't."

"Why not?" He advanced toward me, an Incredible Hulk behaving all sexy—something I'd fantasized about many times. Lifting me up, he pressed me against a bare patch of wall.

"Because . . ." What was I going to say? Oh, yes. "Because there's a ton of snow outside. Your nest would be covered."

"I'd build a glorious nest with a roof and heating and multiple surfaces where I could claim your delectable body."

I liked that he thought I was delectable—too much.

He nudged my legs apart and settled between them like he belonged there. There was nothing I could do but wrap my legs around his waist and cling to his upper arms.

And when he claimed my mouth, I had no interest in doing anything but kissing him back.

CHAPTER 6
VESTALON

I'd lost my wits and my self-control because of this female.

My mate. The thought of possessing her, being with her fully, consumed me.

I ravaged her mouth, and she moaned and jerked her hips toward me, her lips parting and her tongue slipping out to find mine.

I lifted my head. "Bed."

She jerked her head to her right. "Off the living room, first floor."

Lifting her, I tossed her over my shoulder. Mating heat roared through me, and all I could think about was showing this lovely woman that she'd find endless pleasure in my arms.

She might be shocked at how quickly this happened, but it was common with my species. Some orcs might know someone their entire lives, then suddenly the mating heat would rush through them when they were with that person, and they'd both realize this was it. They were fated to be together. Other times, it happened at the first meeting like with me and Emma.

Love and caring always followed.

Everyone knew you'd get to know your fated one while you spent a week or so working through the heat, plus after. This was a welcome thing for orcs, not something to be dreaded.

Inside her bedroom, I nudged the door shut with her pup standing in the hall. He yipped, but I'd make it up to him with pats later. Now was for me and Emma, and I didn't need an audience for what I was going to do with my mate.

I gently laid her on her bed and while it wasn't orc-sized, it was a large surface. We'd fit.

Crawling up over her, I kissed her again, this time savoring how amazing her mouth felt beneath mine, how she clung to my shoulders.

If she was an orc, I'd claim her fully, and she'd welcome that. But Emma was human, and they didn't think or act like an orc. I needed to remember that and make concessions.

I lifted my head and locked my gaze on hers. "I'm going to lick your sweet little clit and make you come."

"Is that a question or a statement?"

"I'm not working hard enough if you have the wits to do more than say yes."

Her lips jerked upward, and that simple gesture was like an arrow embedding itself in my chest. "Perhaps you'd better get back to work then."

"The time to say no is now."

"Let's see how you do in the satisfaction department before I start tossing around full-on commitment."

My mate was witty and gorgeous, and I couldn't wait to claim her fully.

I kissed her sweet mouth again but soon left it, roaming across her jaw and down her neck. I unzipped the top of her odd outfit, taking the fastening all the way to the end near her groin. The garment opened, and I eased the fuzzy orange sleeves from her arms.

A few wiggles, and she'd worked it down around her waist. That would do—for now.

I feathered kisses along her collarbone and between her breasts, sucking in a whiff of her delicious scent. It worked on my pulse like an aphrodisiac, making my heart thunder and my breathing rage.

She was dressed like a fox, but she wore the most delectable undergarments, smooth and silky pink stuff with bits of lace, plus a tiny bow in the center.

"Do you want to remove this, or can I rip through it with my tusks?" I asked, gesturing to her bra.

"As arousing as it might be for you to shred my underwear to get to me, I like this set." Rising a little, she unclipped the bra and tossed it aside, laying back and watching me as I took in her glorious body.

"You're beautiful," I growled.

"My breasts are bigger than I like."

"They're never too big."

"Says a guy. They bounce when I walk."

"I'll watch for that," I said with a grin, stroking a fingertip along the underside of one of her breasts.

"It's hard to find clothing that doesn't make me look lush."

"Lush is good."

"Again, guy."

"I'm all male, sweetheart," I said. "Know that right now."

"I suspected as much."

"Allow me to show you." I sucked one of her nipples into my mouth, and my groan rumbled through my chest. My cock was on fire. I was going to come just from licking her nipple.

I teased her other nipple with my fingers, tugging and rolling it while she moaned and arched her spine to thrust her breast into my mouth.

Leaving her breast, I kissed across her nicely rounded belly, which I adored. She eased out of the rest of her fox attire, kicking it aside, before I could beg to rip through *that* with my tusks. Truly, it was amazing shredding clothing to get to the lush treat beneath.

I spread her legs and crawled between them, tucking my arms beneath her beautifully ripe ass and lifting it, exposing the slick juncture between her legs.

"Wet, just the way I want you, mate," I growled, licking at the sweetness she'd produced from my touch already. "Tell me if there's anything you don't like."

"I . . . Honestly, my ex didn't like doing this, so whatever you do down there is new for me."

I loved that I could be her first for this. I'd make sure it was a memorable moment. A *mating-worthy* moment.

Finding her clit, I ran my tongue across it, then shifted my head back and forth to make my tongue flicker across it.

Moaning, she bucked up to my mouth.

I nibbled on her clit while sliding a finger inside her snug passage. She felt so good. My poor cock throbbed, wanting in on the action.

Maybe next time.

While she panted and gripped the bedding tightly, I licked and sucked on her clit, pushing two fingers inside her and pumping them.

She tasted wonderful, like the storm outside and my salvation. And when she came, I sucked in the flavor.

I'd never do this again with any woman but Emma.

CHAPTER 7
EMMA

Well, our relationship was developing fast. The sexual part of it, that is.

After what happened with my ex, I should bolt out of the house and keep running until I'd forgotten Vestalon existed.

Instead, I laid on the bed in a post-climax stupor, wondering if I could ask him to do it again.

He dropped onto the bed beside me, and the lower part of his legs jutted beyond the end despite his head almost touching the headboard. If he was going to hang around much, I needed to look into orc-sized beds.

No, no, no. I needed to roll off this mattress, walk if I could reconnect my brain to my legs, and pretend it never happened.

He tugged me into his arms and murmured something in a language I hadn't heard before. Orcish? When he kissed the top of my head and snuggled me against his chest, I curled into him, savoring how wonderful it felt to be held.

"I'm sorry if this feels sudden," he said in a gravelly voice.

My laugh spurted out. "We've known each other all of . . . an hour? And now this." I gestured to my naked body. He remained clothed, which was a complete shame.

"As I said, it's common for orcs."

"Explain more about mating heat, if you don't mind."

"Knowledge is power, right?"

"I'm a librarian, so yup."

"Only a few orcs find their true mates, and those are the most fruitful relationships. Others still mate, or marry in human terms, with someone they'll care for, though they're lucky to produce one orcling. Those who find their true mates are almost immediately overcome with a heat. It ensures survival of the species. During the heat, they'll mate numerous times. The heat eventually fades."

"What if their true mate doesn't wish to initiate or continue the relationship?"

He stilled, holding his breath. "It's rare, but if the other person doesn't want a true mating, the one going into heat will go to a cave within the orc kingdom that's reserved for such a time. He'll remain there until the heat wanes. After that, he'll avoid the other person to keep from triggering his heat again."

"Sounds unpleasant."

"I imagine it is. It's rare for anyone to reject a fated

mate. They're your perfect match, the one you're destined to spend your life with. The couples are exceedingly happy."

"For those who choose not to pursue the relationship, do they go on to find new true mates?"

"Sadly, no."

"I'm not saying I'm rejecting you," I said softly.

"I'm grateful to hear that."

"I wouldn't want to be responsible for sending you to a cave where you'll . . . I assume you'll spend a lot of time jerking off."

"It's that or suffer."

I rolled over to face him. I loved how he smelled and how earnestly he watched me, as if I could hand him everything or rip him apart with only one word. "You don't love me. How could you?"

"That's the thing. Because you're my fated mate, I know I will love you, and that's a blessing."

"Love can hurt."

"Only if you're with the wrong person."

He sounded so sure about that. "How does this make you feel? I'm not playing psychiatrist here, but this heat appears to be solely on your end."

"So says the woman who let me carry her into her bedroom and eat her out within an hour of meeting her."

"Touché."

"A heat impacts us both. One is the primary, so to speak, which in this case is me. Closeness will cause a similar reaction in the second person."

"You're saying I'll have the equivalent of a hard-on the more time I spend with you?"

"You'll crave me, but it's not frightening because I'll feel the same. I'll be happy to take care of your needs."

"I'm sure you would. Look, I mentioned an ex. While it's been a year, I'm not sure I'm ready for another relationship yet."

"You have time to think about this."

"How long?"

"When the storm's over, I'll ask you for a decision."

"What's the offer on the table?" I asked.

"We continue the mating, or you'll tell me you're not interested."

"What will you do if I say no?"

"Find a cave in the orc kingdom and ride it out."

CHAPTER 8

VESTALON

"I mentioned I'm a businessmale," I said as we prepared dinner in her kitchen. We hadn't talked more about matings, but she'd given me a nod at my suggestion for how we should handle this. "I'm used to being in control, telling others what to do, and preparing myself for any issues that might come up."

She handed me a package of carrots and a cucumber from the fridge to add to the salad I was making while she prepped some potatoes and steak. She'd lit the grill on the back deck after I shoveled it clear, and I'd offered to cook the meat. The awning kept most of the snow from settling, but it was cold outside.

I didn't want my mate to get chilly.

Although warming her up would be a lot of fun.

"Control's a good thing except in relationships." She shot me an odd look. "I'm more a give and take kind of person. My ex was a jerk. He cheated on me and then announced we were divorcing so he could marry his latest. I thought we were in it for forever. While I was, he sure wasn't."

"You'll have a hard time trusting someone new." I dumped the finely chopped carrots into the bowl and started on the cucumber.

"I guess so."

"That's the norm. Burned once, twice avoiding fire. Something like that."

She stared down at the steaks. "I'm gun shy, but who can blame me?"

"Do you still love him?" I needed to know what I was competing with here. A ghost of a guy who wasn't what she'd believed?

"No. Let's face it, when someone cheats, it eventually cauterizes the love you hold close to your heart. Now I wonder if I ever loved him. How could I when he wasn't the guy I thought I fell for?"

"I guess it comes down to whether you're willing to try again."

"I'm lonely." She shot me a longing glance. "I want children, and I want to be with someone who cares as much for me as I do him."

"I can work with that."

"I can't believe you're already all in."

I shrugged. "This could be the mating heat speaking, but it's also the norm for orcs. I grew up with the idea of possibly finding my true mate and being with her forever, so I'm not intimidated by the notion."

"You said we have until the storm ends."

"We do."

Her smile loosened the tension on her face. "Then let's decide everything then."

"Alright."

As I'd told her, I was a businessmale. Cutthroat, some might say, though I'd never done anything underhanded to win.

"Know right now, mate," I said, "I'm going to do all I can to make sure you say yes."

CHAPTER 9
EMMA

"I'll sleep on the sofa," I said as we were getting ready for bed.

"I can sleep there," he said. "It's longer than your bed. My feet will dangle over the end of the bed."

"But the bed's more comfortable."

He shrugged. "The sofa will be fine."

"We could share." I said bravely. "We don't need to do anything."

"There's no way I'm sleeping in a bed with you, Emma, without doing *something*."

"Yup, then I'll take the sofa. You can sleep at an angle on the bed, and then your feet won't hang off the end."

He grumbled. "There's no way I'm letting you give up your bed for me."

"I offered."

"And I say no."

We could argue all night, or I could give in. I didn't want to bicker with him. I liked him a lot, and I wanted to see where this might end up between us. Squabbling with him wouldn't take us anywhere.

"Okay," I said, heading into the bathroom. "I'll get ready, and you can have the bathroom after me. I'll put a toothbrush on the sink for you. I always keep a spare."

"Why?"

"In case someone needs to stay over, and they don't bring one with them."

He frowned but said nothing.

"I don't sleep around, contrary to what we did earlier in my bedroom. But I have friends and two sisters. They come to stay sometimes."

"I'm not jealous," he growled. "Not too much. I have no reason to feel that way, so I'm going to push that emotion aside."

I paused in the open bathroom doorway. "Is it that easy?"

"I'm going to try."

With a nod, I went inside and got ready, changing into a nightie while I was there. When I emerged, he sat on the sofa, staring at the fire that was dying down again. I'd let it go out.

"The bathroom's all yours," I said.

"Thank you." He came over to stand in front of me. "Your hair's lovely."

I'd brushed it and left it free. "I don't cut it often, though I've thought about it."

"You should wear it the way you want to, but I adore the length."

Now I wasn't sure I'd ever cut it, though he was right. I'd do what I wanted with my own body.

"Good night. I'll see you in the morning." I wasn't sure what I read in his golden eyes. A bit of longing mixed in with something I couldn't define—something I didn't want to examine closely because the feeling could be mirrored in me.

I eased around him and with Milo trotting at my heels, went inside my bedroom, nudging the door almost closed behind me.

Milo hopped up onto the bed and stared at the door, whining.

"He's not sleeping with us," I whispered. "Get that idea out of your head right now."

With a huff, he settled on the blankets, dropping his chin onto his front paws, watching the door.

I climbed under the covers and turned out the light.

Sleep was a long time coming.

THE NEXT MORNING, I hurried into the bathroom, still half asleep. Milo trotted in with me and put his paws up on the side of the tub. While I did my thing, Milo tugged back the curtain, revealing a completely naked orc standing in the shower.

"Ah," I cried.

Vestalon grinned and kept spraying his big green cock with the hand-held shower. "Like the view?"

I covered my eyes with my hands. "I'm sorry. I don't

know why I didn't hear the water running." Because I had to pee, and I was still sleepy. Wiping quickly, I stood and yanked my nightie down over my thighs. "I'll, um, get out of here and leave you to finish."

"I'd be happy to let you finish this for me." He nudged his chiseled chin to the hand sprayer.

His cock had started to rise, and it was a thick thing with nubs along the sides that would rub just right. It had a thick head that would stretch me as he pushed it hard inside me, though I imagined I'd be so saturated by then; I'd be able to take that part at least with one thrust.

Why was I thinking that this was inevitable?

"I've got a spur," he said. "And I knot."

"Excuse me?" And why was I stepping toward the shower, eager to take the sprayer and aim it?

"Spur. It rubs your clit while I thrust inside you."

Damn, how could simple talk like this turn me on?

"And I'll knot after I come."

"What exactly does that mean?" I'd heard of wolves knotting but— "Oh, you mean the base will swell and you'll remain locked inside me for a period of time."

"Not the base. In my species, it's the head."

When I imagined it swelling, locking within me, my spine went melty, and my body slicked with excitement.

"This ensures my seed finds whatever your body has to offer. Sure you don't want to discover what it's like?"

"I can't believe you're offering something like that." Now I sounded like a prude. My body was humming, eager to try out spurs and knotting. "I'm leaving," I said with a huff.

He laughed as I scooted from the bathroom with Milo.

Inside my bedroom, Milo jumped back up on the bed. He circled around in my warm spot and laid down, sighing.

"You were a naughty boy doing that to us," I said.

Milo gave me a doggie grin.

I grunted and sat on the bed, cupping my hot face with my palms. It was a long time before I felt ready to leave the bedroom.

When I opened the door, the smell of bacon and coffee greeted me.

A male who can cook? If Vestalon kept this up, I'd be in love with him before noon.

Just kidding, but still.

I scooted into the bathroom and took a shower, tugging a long-sleeved red dress over my head and smoothing it across my thighs afterward. My bare feet made almost no sound as I entered the living room and closed the damper on the fireplace. I'd clean the ashes out later, and we could have another fire tonight.

I paused in the entrance to the kitchen, watching as Vestalon worked at the stove, carefully removing slices of cooked bacon from a pan and placing them on a paper towel to drain. He cracked eggs and they sizzled when they hit the fat left over in the frying pan.

"I took the liberty of making breakfast." He glanced over his shoulder. "I hope you're hungry."

What, he wasn't offering his spur and knot as the first course?

Maybe I was the naughty one, not Milo.

My dog sat beside me, looking from Vestalon to me. He nudged my calf with his nose, urging me to approach Vestalon.

"Don't," I hissed.

Vestalon sent me a brow-raised look before turning back to the stove.

"You're not wearing your suit." In fact, he wore low-slung gray sweatpants and one of my aprons to protect his naked chest.

Damn, his back and shoulders were nice, a landscape of rippling muscles I was eager to traverse.

Turning, he leaned against the counter, showing off acres of gorgeous green skin and my apron emblazoned with Kiss the Cook across the front. I was sorely tempted to take him up on the offer. "I had a workout bag in my truck. I went down this morning to grab it. I didn't want to put my old stuff on after showering."

A quick glance out the window confirmed my suspicion. "It's still storming."

"The road's not far."

"You could've been hurt."

"I promise, I watched where I was going, and I didn't fall. Milo went with me." He squatted down to pat my dog. "Didn't you, little guy? Enjoyed it too, right?" He scratched behind Milo's ears and my pup ate up the affection. "My truck's still impaling your poor tree, and no one's plowed the road."

"They don't often come by until after the storm's over."

"What if you have an emergency?"

"They'll send a state truck to clear the way for an ambulance."

My pup plopped on the ground, rolled onto his back, and presented Vestalon with his belly, which Vestalon promptly rubbed.

I kinda wanted to go lay on the floor and see what he could do for my belly . . . And areas below my belly.

I was completely in lust with Vestalon.

How could I resist his lure?

CHAPTER 10

VESTALON

"What would you like to do today?" Emma asked as we washed the dishes together.

"I retrieved my laptop from my truck. I should work."

Her lips pursed, but she said nothing.

"What?" I asked with lifted brows.

"It's snowing. Christmas is almost here. And you want to work?"

"I don't necessarily *want* to work, but I should."

"What will happen if you don't?"

I had to think about that for a moment. "Not much, I suppose. While orcs don't celebrate Christmas, many of my staff do. The office is closed until after the new year."

"You're a generous boss." She handed me the last dish to dry.

I buffed it with the towel and placed it inside the cupboard with the others. "Why generous?"

"I've heard of giving everyone the day off but never

all the way through New Year's. I had to take vacation time to be off myself."

"My employees want to be with their families and friends."

"What about you?" Turning, she leaned her hip against the counter, looking up at me.

I shrugged. "I can see my family pretty much whenever I want. My half-brother, Thraal, lives a few towns over. He mated with a human, Autumn."

"I think I heard something about them. They're both high school teachers, right?"

"They are. Jarum and Kassia also teach and mated."

"Lots of mating going on."

I grinned. "That's why so many orcs emerged from the mountain. With few females, we need to look elsewhere for mates."

"Did you hope to find a mate among we humans?"

"I didn't plan on it." I advanced on her, pinning her against the island with my palms on either side of her hips. Her sudsy hands fluttered against my chest. "It happened. You're mine. All mine." A growl ripped through me, and my cock shot to attention. The look she'd given me while I stood naked in her shower still haunted me.

She craved me as much as I did her.

"It's happening again, isn't it?" she said.

I frowned. "What's happening?"

"Your heat's growing. And here you wanted to grab that laptop and get to work." The tease gliding through her voice made me want her even more.

"You're probably right."

"Just probably?" Leaning back, she traced a fingertip down my erection pressing against the front of my sweatpants, and just like she'd hit a switch, I was all over her.

Pivoting, I swiped everything off the island. I lifted and laid her on the now-empty surface and loomed over her.

"I will say, that when the heat's upon you, you're rather sexy," she said, all husky and with dilated pupils.

"Only *rather* sexy?" I grumbled.

She caressed my shoulders and wrapped her legs around me. I wanted her like this while I plunged inside her.

"I'll concede you're *very* sexy."

"Good girl." I flipped up her skirt and gulped when I saw the thread of underwear she wore beneath. "My, my, my. You're a *very* good girl."

"Only very?" she quipped.

A flick of my finger, and one of my retractable claws extended. I held it up. "I'm going to slice through that bit of cloth you call underwear, then consume you."

"You seem to do a lot of talking and not enough action."

She was egging me on, and I loved it.

I grinned and severed her underwear, pushing it aside.

Then I spread her legs and dove between them, licking first her wet opening and then focusing on her clit. I sucked on it, twirling my tongue across it while she writhed on the counter. She gripped my horns tight, and then stroked them, which only drove me wilder.

With her legs propped over my shoulders, I drove my tongue inside her while running my fingers across her clit. She bucked, whimpering with need.

My cock was on fire, and I'd give anything to drive it inside her.

For now, pleasing her in this way would keep my heat in check. My cock would ache, but it could deal. Loving Emma like this was important, because it showed me how to please her.

When I plunged my fingers inside her, making sure I stroked her G-Spot, she cried out, lifting her hips to meet my hand.

She came apart suddenly, arching her spine and milking my fingers.

I continued to lick her clit.

I didn't stop until she collapsed back onto the counter.

"THE WEATHER OUTSIDE IS FRIGHTFUL," Emma sang along with music piped in from the television. "But the fire is so delightful." A fake crackling fire played on the screen, and the setting for a real one waited to be lit in the fireplace. "Let it snow, let it snow, let it snow." Rising from where she did something while sitting on the sofa with scissors and paper, she danced over to where I sat working on my computer.

I was trying to work, that is. All I'd done so far was log onto the internet and stare at the screen.

Pausing beside me, Emma continued to hum and sway her hips while slowly unfolding the snipped-up piece of paper.

"Voila," she announced, lifting her creation in the air. "I think I should start hanging them from thread in the kitchen, don't you?"

"What is it?"

She held it close to my face. "A paper snowflake. See?"

"It's pretty. Definitely make more and hang them in the kitchen."

That was the right thing to say. She grinned and sashayed around the living room, her snowflake held aloft, singing about Santa baby coming down her chimney tonight.

I wished *I* could come down her chimney tonight.

She danced from the room and returned a bit later without her snowflakes. "They look nice. Come see." Taking my hand, she dragged me up from the hassock I was sitting on and into her kitchen, pointing. "See? See? Gorgeous, right?"

"Perfect." They actually looked amazing, dancing like she continued to do from the soft air currents swirling through the open room.

"You should help me with my next project." She frowned. "Unless you still have work to do."

"What's the next project?"

"I want to make a paper chain and drape it around the living room."

"What's a paper chain?"

"I'm glad you asked." She took my hand again and tugged me back into the living room, Milo yipping and wiggling beside her as she sang about trimming her tree with decorations from Tiffanys, whoever that was.

She tugged me down onto the sofa beside her.

"Here." She gave me a few pieces of red and green paper, plus scissors. "Cut these into thin strips, like this." She showed me, and it wasn't difficult. "When we've made all the strips, we'll link them together."

In no time, we'd constructed a very long chain, piling it onto the floor between us.

"Time to hang it up," she announced, rising from the sofa and holding the end of the chain aloft. "Can you boost me so I can tape it near the ceiling?"

With Milo hopping along with us, we started in the far corner, Emma securing the chain to the highest part of the wall, me holding her so she could reach.

We'd nearly made it around the room when Milo suddenly jumped in front of me.

I toppled to the floor, twisting to avoid landing on the pup while taking the brunt of the fall.

Rolling, I came to a stop lying on top of Emma.

CHAPTER 11
EMMA

"You're making a habit of this," I said with a grin.

"I am. Thoughts?"

"I like it."

"You're not hurt, are you?" Vestalon's gaze locked onto my lips.

"Nope. You?"

He shook his head.

"What happened?" I asked.

"Milo jumped in front of me. I didn't want to step on him, but I lost my footing and . . . here we are."

I huffed, though I wasn't upset. "That Milo." My pup, who was sitting nearby, his head swiveling back and forth between us, rose and wagged his fluffy tail.

Was he playing matchmaker? Nah. It wasn't possible, was it?

"I suppose I should get off you," Vestalon said.

"Only if you wish."

"I'd rather stay here all day, then." Lowering his head, he kissed me.

I drank in his taste—with hints of the mulled cider we'd been drinking—and the wonderful feel of his weight lying across my body. I held his shoulders, wishing we were lying in my bed, wearing nothing.

I was falling in love with Vestalon, and it felt amazing.

He lifted his head. "I'm falling in love with you, Emma. You need to know that."

"I . . . feel the same."

With a growl, he kissed me again, his tongue teasing across mine. We didn't come up for air until Milo yipped and raced to the front door to go outside.

"Do you want me to take him out?" Vestalon asked. "Or continue to lie on top of you."

"Stay on top of me."

Milo barked and scampered over to wiggle beside us before running to the door again.

"It appears your pup has other ideas."

So much for playing matchmaker.

"I can go outside," he said. "It'll give me a chance to cool down."

His hard erection pressed against my knee, and now that I'd seen it, it was all I could think about. Human guys had nothing on orcs with spurs. And knotting? While I was on the pill and couldn't get pregnant, I'd like to practice in case I decided to ditch birth control.

Wait, was I seriously contemplating having an orcling with Vestalon?

I was.

Maybe I was also in heat. What did I want to do about it?

"You don't have a coat or boots," I said in a strangled voice. My mind was zipping in all directions and each path led to me and Vestalon, naked.

"I'll clear the walkway again while I'm out there." Rising, he held his hand out to me to tug me up from the floor.

My body was coiled tight, needing release, but Milo deserved to go out when he had the need. "If you keep doing things like this, I'm going to want to keep you around forever."

He smiled and strode to the door. "Then I'd better get started."

He leashed Milo and stepped outside—dressed only in sweats and his work shoes, his chest still bare.

By the time he came back inside, I'd composed myself. My clit still throbbed, but I'd suppressed my urge to do a striptease for Vestalon and drag him off to my bedroom.

We made dinner and ate it at the island, him standing because he didn't fit in any of my chairs.

Afterward, we sat together on the living room sofa, Milo coiled up between us. We'd started the fire, and I'd made Vestalon his first cup of hot cocoa.

He took a tentative sip and grimaced.

"If you don't like it, you don't have to drink it," I said.

"It's sweet."

I grinned. "And that's why I love it. Chocolate, sweetness, and the mini marshmallows only make it better."

"I'm not saying I don't like it."

"Do you enjoy chocolate?"

"I'm not sure I've ever had it before."

I frowned. "How long have you lived among humans?"

"A year. We grow cocoa beans in the hills surrounding the biggest orc city, so orcs eat chocolate too."

"Just not you."

He huffed and shook his head. "We grow coffee beans too, plus tea. If you visit the kingdom, you'll find we're very similar in manners and tastes."

"And yet you haven't tried chocolate." I sighed. "That's pretty much a sin."

"From what I've heard about humans, sin usually involves sex."

"*Some* of the seven deadly sins involve sex." I ticked them off on my finger. "Pride, greed, wrath, envy, lust, gluttony, and sloth."

"In this, orcs and humans are also similar. We're raised to believe we shouldn't be too prideful. Greed's frowned upon. Envy's natural, don't you think?"

"As long as you don't let it control what you do, I'd say it's the least harmful sin."

"I imagine there are as many gluttonous orcs as humans. And sloth. Hmm. I work *too* much."

"Reconsidering your job choice?"

"I love what I do, but lately, I've been thinking all

those hours aren't sustainable. I've achieved the goals I set for myself. I have more money than I can ever imagine spending. And the thrill of winning all the time has waned. Like you, I want orclings and someone to be with. I want to have fun."

"Life's much too short, as everyone says. You don't want to wake up when you're seventy and realize you didn't take time to do all the things you dreamed about."

"It's not too late even at seventy."

"I don't think one hundred is too late to have fun, but you know what I mean."

His brow scrunched. "I understand."

My brain shot to all the fun we could have in bed, but I again suppressed the urge to strip and climb onto his lap. Impale myself on his cock. Show him what it was like when I let the sin of lust consume me.

"It's almost Christmas," I choked out. "It's probably not safe to go sledding or skiing, but we can do some fun things inside. Do you like cookies?"

"I eat them all."

I laughed. "I happen to have a batch of dough in the fridge I need to roll out, cut into holiday shapes, bake, and decorate. You can help me with them and after, we can eat them."

He grinned. "They don't need to be decorated for me to enjoy them."

"It's part of the fun."

"They'll be gone in no time. Truly, they can be mounds of dough and it doesn't matter to me what they look like as long as they taste good."

"It's part of the process."

Milo looked between us before releasing a satisfied puppy sigh. He dropped his chin onto his paws, and his eyelids slid shut.

"Decorating it is, then," Vestalon said. "What else can we do?"

"Watch Christmas shows on TV. There are some favorites I have to see each year."

"I don't believe I've ever watched one."

"Do you have similar holidays?"

"The Hostedeer Festival is quite popular in the kingdom. It takes place over three days, and we feast on traditional dishes to celebrate the harvest. The Festival culminates in a dance under the moonlight on the very last night."

"It sounds lovely."

"We dance naked."

I lifted my eyebrows. "Everyone?"

"We send the orclings to bed first. Sometimes, the dancing gets . . ."

"Steamy?"

"We're not exhibitionists," he insisted gravely.

"Of course not."

"But things *can* become heated."

I couldn't imagine doing something like that. "Humans, for the most part, keep their clothing on during festivals."

His eyes sparkled. "How sad for you."

"Back to the sins. What about wrath?"

He shrugged and shot me a rueful smile. "I'm an orc.

Wrath's bred into our bones. While the kingdom's settled and clans rarely feud, as a species, we'll probably never fully set wrath aside."

"One could say the same thing about humans. Wars are still fought and even on a local level, feuds continue."

He took another sip of his cocoa and frowned down at the marshmallows bobbing across the surface. "I still don't see how chocolate can be considered sinful."

"We say that because it's decadent."

"No one would kill to possess it."

"I hope not, though if we were down to the last chocolate bar on the planet, I'd fight you for it."

"I'd win."

"Don't forget my taekwondo."

"Show me your moves, mate."

"Later."

He pretended to scowl. "You were joking about knowing martial arts."

I grinned. "Behave and you'll never find out."

"I could see the sinful properties if I drizzled this cocoa all over your body and licked it off."

I sputtered, trying again not to succumb to the lust swirling inside me. All I could think about was me daring him and him doing it. Who cared about being sticky when it came to something like him licking cocoa off my body?

"I'm getting the feeling you like my idea, sweetheart," he growled, lowering his cocoa onto the coffee table. "I saw online the storm will end by tomorrow."

"Have you considered spending the rest of the time

having sex?" A thrill shot through me, and my clit throbbed.

"If you're open to the idea, I'm game."

"You're in heat. Of course you're game."

"What about you?"

Confession time. "I believe I'm in heat too."

CHAPTER 12
VESTALON

"What did you say?" I growled, my cock slamming against my abs.

"I have this insatiable urge to climb all over you—naked."

She climbed into my lap and stroked my chest. I rubbed circles on her bare thighs, nudging up her dress with each pass.

I was about to undo my pants and shuck them when Milo hopped up onto the sofa behind us, startling us both. He held a sprig of something in his mouth and thrust it against my shoulder.

I stare at it. So did Emma.

"What's that?" I asked.

"Mistletoe." Laughter bubbled in her voice. "I believe my pup is playing matchmaker."

"Do we need one?"

"I'm beginning to think that's a no."

Milo barked and nudged my shoulder with it again.

"What's mistletoe?" I asked.

"A parasitic shrub, though I think we forget about what it actually is during the holidays. It's a traditional Christmas thing. If a couple finds themselves beneath a sprig, they're supposed to kiss. If they don't, it's considered bad luck."

"I wouldn't want to give either of us bad luck."

"Nope." Her lips quirked up on one side.

I kissed her, and she moaned, running her fingertips across my chest. I started thinking about drizzling cocoa across her body again.

In no time, we were tugging at each other's clothing, removing everything.

"We're naked," she said with a gasp, looking me up and down. Her attention homed in on my erect cock thrusting up between us. The sweet vulnerability in her eyes made my heart seize. "I want you."

"I'm yours already." I swept her off her feet and strode into her bedroom, where I kicked the door shut and laid her on the blankets.

She stared up at me. "I wasn't sure I'd ever trust someone new again. But I trust you, Vestalon. I know you won't hurt me."

"Never," I vowed. How could I? She was my true mate, the one I'd adore for the rest of my days.

I feasted my eyes on her body, so lush and curvy, before climbing over her, bracing my weight above her.

When I claimed her mouth with my own, she moaned and dug her nails into my shoulders.

I kissed my way down her body, pausing to lavish her

breasts with attention. I teased them with my tongue and lips, stroking them until she was panting and writhing beneath me.

"You have the most beautiful breasts," I murmured as I moved lower still. "I've got big hands and you fill them. So perfect."

She laughed softly, the sound of it making me smile against her skin.

I licked and sucked her nipples until she was panting with pleasure.

"Vestalon," she gasped as I moved lower, kissing my way down her stomach to the juncture of her thighs. "You make me feel good."

I continued my exploration with my tongue. Her taste was sweet and salty, and it made me hungrier for more of her. When I finally looked up at her face again, she had tears in her eyes. "What is it? Did I do something wrong?"

She shook her head and reached for me. "You do everything right, Vestalon. You make me feel beautiful and loved and cherished like no one else ever has before."

"He hurt you."

She nodded.

"I'll kill him."

"Don't bother. He's not worth risking your life."

"You think he'd prove a challenge to me?"

"Not a bit, but humans frown on things like that. You could get in trouble."

"Then I'll rip his arms off instead."

Her laugh snorted out, but I wasn't joking. "Again,

don't bother. He's not worth even one thought on your part."

"I want to get revenge for you," I said. "Make him suffer because he's making you sad."

"Just telling me you'd do this for me is enough."

"Not quite." I flashed her a smile. "Licking you will probably help."

"Maybe give it a try and we'll find out?" she said, the imp. At least she wasn't crying any longer. That was ripping my lungs straight out of my body.

I smiled and kissed her again, feeling the growing affection between us. It wasn't just her or me facing whatever came next, but us.

I dove back down between her legs, licking and sucking on her clit until she was trembling with anticipation. Her cries grew louder as I teased her sensitive bud. I explored every inch of her passage with my fingers, learning what made her gasp and moan and beg for more.

But when she started to clench around me, I stopped, drawing back so that she wouldn't reach the peak of pleasure without me.

Crawling up her body, I kissed her gently. "Not yet, my love, but soon." I rolled her over, on to her belly, and lifted her hips. "Can I take you this way, mate?" I asked with a growl. My cock throbbed, engorged with my heat.

"Please do," she said over her shoulder.

I placed the head of my cock at her entrance and, holding her hips, pushed myself deep inside her.

CHAPTER 13
EMMA

is cock was thick and long. As he pushed himself inside me, the nubs along the sides quivered. When he pulled out and drove himself back into me, I was suddenly saturated, as if the nubs also secreted lubrication.

"You're with me, mate?" he asked, his voice deep and husky.

"All the way, Vestalon. Claim me. Show me this heat of yours and don't stop until it starts to wane."

"That could take a week or more," he said with a low chuckle.

"The storm outside might end, but the one that's brewing between us is just beginning."

He thrust into me again, the sensation of his thick cock pushing against my inner walls, stretching them fully. His hands gripped my hips, holding me in place as he moved steadily in and out of me. I shoved back against him, driving him deeper while savoring the heat radiating from his body.

My breathing grew heavier with each thrust, and I began to match him stroke for stroke. Our bodies moved together in perfect harmony, our moans of pleasure echoing in my small bedroom.

The nubs massaged my inner walls as he thrust, and my brain started spiraling.

His spur must've wrapped around his cock, because it found my clit. It latched on and sucked, and it was all I could do not to explode that instant.

Not yet, I told my body. *I want to feel more.*

His breath was hot against my neck, and he kissed me there, whispering words of love and adoration that only made me want him more. He went faster, pushing harder; an unstoppable force that brought us both to the brink of ecstasy before finally letting us fall into its depths together.

I came all at once, and his shout echoed my groan. He rode my orgasm while giving into his own.

Finally, he slowed. He stroked my back and sides and cupped my ass. "Beautiful," he murmured. "So perfect." Easing to the side, he took me with him, tumbling us down onto the bed.

"You're tight inside me. That must be your knot. You should know that I'm on the pill."

"Orc sperm find a way."

My laugh burst out. "We'll see about that." I liked the full feeling of his knot, however. It was a delicious bonus.

We lay there in contentment, basking in the afterglow. Ripples of pleasure shot through me, followed by a twitch of his cock.

"Knotting still?" I asked.

"I'll remain inside you for a bit, but soon, I'll start to stiffen again."

"I can look forward to this all night?"

"If you wish."

"I do."

That's when I knew I was falling into true love for the first time in my life.

CHAPTER 14
VESTALON

I woke before Emma the next morning—to bright sunshine streaming in through the bedroom window. The storm was over.

What did that mean for us?

Not wanting to think about it, I showered, scrunching over to keep from hitting my head on the ceiling, and dressed in my second pair of sweats and a t-shirt. When I packed my gym bag, I never would've dreamed I'd be tugging on the clothing inside my true mate's home.

Emma continued to sleep, but Milo followed me into the kitchen, looking forlornly from the back door with sunlight poking in through the window, to me, and toward the bedroom.

I fed him and put his leash on, stuffing my feet into my shoes.

Outside, we were greeted by a winter wonderland. Since the snow was so deep, I released Milo from his leash. He was much too small to make his way through the drifts to the road. He hopped around, floundering in the snow, woofing as he stuffed his nose into it.

I cleared the walkway; grateful I'd kept it relatively clear during the storm.

After Milo had done his business, I put him back inside and tackled the path I'd created down the driveway earlier.

As I cleared around my truck, a plow passed on the road. The driver stopped and got out.

"Hey, are you alright?" He took in my truck still impaling the tree. "That's quite an accident right there."

"I'm fine. It happened a few days ago. I've been sheltering at the house up this driveway." I gestured in the general direction. "I don't suppose you know of anyone with a tow truck who could come pick up my vehicle and take it into town where I can look into repairs, do you?"

"I sure do." He pulled his phone. "An orc like you owns a business in town. He does body work, too, and after your insurance company comes to look at the truck, I bet he could do the repairs for you." After dialing, he frowned, listening. When the other person picked up, he explained the situation and ended the call. "You're in luck. He's not far from here right now, and he'll swing by this way and collect your vehicle. Will you wait with it?"

"Yes."

The driver got back into his plow truck and continued down the road, shoving snow into the ditch. I climbed into my truck and checked my phone, grateful to see I had a signal.

I sent Emma a text, explaining what was going on, ending with, *Miss you already. Love you. Keep the bed warm...*

She didn't reply, but she was probably still asleep. After my truck was in town, I'd hitch a ride back here, picking up coffee and donuts on the way.

My half-brother, Thraal, answered on the second ring. "Hey, Vestalon. You're alive!"

"Sorry I couldn't reach out to you," I said. "I went off the road at the beginning of the storm on the way home from visiting my grandmother." He and I shared the same mother, but this grandmother was my dad's mom. She moved here from the orc kingdom to open a pizza place after sampling and loving a fellow orc's mate's pizza. Kassia had visited the orc kingdom with her new mate, Jarum. She'd passed his mother's orc mating tests and introduced pizza to the orc world. It was a hit, and my grandmother had come up with a twist to the recipe she now shared with humans.

"You said you went off the road?" Thraal said. "Are you okay?"

"I'm fine. I . . ." I still couldn't quite believe what happened, but the low hum in my body told me it was all true. "I was rescued by my true mate. We—"

"Hey, congratulations!"

"Her name's Emma, and she's amazing."

"Human I assume?"

"Yup. It seems we both have a thing for them," I said with a chuckle.

"We do. I don't know where I'd be without Autumn."

Hiding out in a cave while waiting for his heat to wane, I supposed. Me too.

"Anyway. She let me stay at her house—"

Thraal barked out a laugh. "I can only imagine how that went."

"She's an understanding woman."

"I'm happy for you, Vestalon," he said softly. "You deserve the best."

"We both do, and we've found it."

"You're right."

I explained about the tow truck, which I could already hear coming down the road.

"Will you go into town with him to fill out paperwork?"

"Yeah. I let Emma know what's happening."

"I'd offer to meet you at the body shop, but me and Autumn decided to head to North Conway. We're holed up at Moat Mountain and they've only begun to dig us out."

"It's okay, I'll figure something out."

"Let me know when you're back in town. We can set up dinner. I'd love to meet Emma."

"Will do."

We hung up as the tow truck pulled up beside me, and the driver soon had my vehicle secured on the back.

"I need to go tell my . . . my mate," Damn, it felt good to call her that, "what's happening. Do you have a few minutes to wait?"

"Sure," he said, tapping his fingers on his steering wheel in time with the low music playing on the radio.

"Hurry it up, though. Yours isn't the first vehicle in need of a tow."

I skidded up the driveway and went inside, striding to the bedroom. Emma still slept, and I'd never seen anyone prettier in my life than my mate deep in slumber. We'd worn each other out last night. I'd let her keep sleeping.

In the kitchen, I wrote a note. Not sure where to leave it, I grinned and strode into the living room, placing it beneath one of our cold cups of cocoa from last night. She'd smile when she saw it, because I alluded to all the things I couldn't wait to do with her when I got back, including baking and decorating cookies, kissing under the mistletoe, and getting creative with some warm cocoa.

I'd found my holiday spirit, and it came from the woman I loved.

Before I left, I stooped down and called Milo over, giving him lots of pats. "Make sure Emma sees my note, will you, little guy?"

Milo seemed to nod, which was good enough for me.

After tugging on my suit jacket, I grabbed my bag and hurried back down the driveway.

CHAPTER 15
EMMA

I woke and stretched out muscles that had gotten a solid workout last night, smiling despite the ache.

Vestalon was no longer in the bed with me, but I suspected he was somewhere about. Hopefully, he'd made coffee.

The sun was out, which meant the storm was over. I was a little nervous about what that might mean for us. Not about us being together. True mates didn't end things that easily. I was confident our relationship would only get better.

But where would we live? Vestalon had a full life in the city, and I was happy here in my snug home and with my job at the library. Would he want to move in with me or would he expect me to give up everything that made me the person I'd become? If he asked, could I find a way to fit into his city life?

Rising, I slipped into the bathroom, brushed my

teeth, and took a shower. At least the power hadn't failed during the storm.

When I emerged dressed, I strode to the kitchen, not finding Vestalon there. Milo trotted over to me and sat. I bypassed him and went to the living room.

"Vestalon?" He wasn't there either, or in the dining room. I doubted he'd gone to the basement, and when I opened the front door and peered outside, I found he'd cleared the walkway and part of the drive. Maybe he was down at his truck.

The roar of a plow rang out, and my friend pushed snow to the side, slowly making his way up my driveway to my house.

I waited inside until he was nearly finished, then went out to pay him, which I insisted on doing despite him offering to do this as a friend.

"Hey, thanks," I said, handing it to him.

"Aw, you don't have to pay me, sweetheart," the withered, gray-haired man said, scratching the back of his neck.

"I insist. You're so nice to do this. It would take me hours to clear it with my snowblower."

"Well, I thank you kindly." He tossed the cash up onto the dashboard of his truck.

"You didn't happen to see an orc around, did you?" I asked.

Frowning, he shook his head. "Can't say that I have."

"Maybe he's in his truck."

"Truck?"

"The one that hit the tree at the end of my drive."

Ray's frown deepened, and he glanced over his shoulder. "There's no truck at the end of the driveway, either."

Huh. Vestalon must've called for a tow.

"Thanks again," I said, backing away from the vehicle.

"Any time, sweetheart." He waved and backed down the drive.

Unease spilled through me as I went back inside.

"Vestalon just went into town to arrange to have his truck repaired. He'll be back."

I made breakfast—enough for two. Long after it got cold, I ate my share and put the leftovers in the fridge. I'd warm them up when he got back.

My phone remained silent. He had my number. He'd send me a message.

Sighing, I went to the living room and turned on the TV, where I scrolled through the fifty billion channels but didn't find anything I wanted to watch. Even Rudolph didn't hold appeal. As the day wore on, Milo sat beside me, staring my way, but I couldn't bear to look at him. All I could see was Vestalon playing with my pup and how much Milo enjoyed having Vestalon scratch behind his ears.

Vestalon didn't show up by lunchtime.

Or dinnertime.

Or, sigh, bedtime.

"How can I go to bed without him?" I asked the living room in general.

Milo woofed, but that was no explanation for Vestalon's absence.

I shut the TV off and went into the kitchen with Milo tap-tap-tapping behind me.

Taking the cookie dough from the fridge, I rolled it out and cut shapes. Bells, gingerbread women, and a few Christmas trees.

My eyes kept watering, and I swiped my tears away. I wouldn't cry about a guy ever again.

While the cookies baked, I mixed up the icing and dug the colored sprinkles out of the drawer.

"Red and green, right, Milo?"

My pup didn't reply.

Sniffing some more, I fed him and refreshed his water. I took the cookies out of the oven and placed them on the cooling rack.

Vestalon still hadn't come home.

"Home?" I said with a hint of self-mockery. "This isn't *his* home. He has a home and a full life in the city."

Maybe he didn't want to share it with me.

"No, no, no," I chided myself. "You trust him. He's honest and true, and he wouldn't screw you and bail."

I repeated the words over and over as I decorated the cookies, coating each with colorful sprinkles.

Finally, I couldn't find an excuse to delay going to bed.

As I brushed my teeth, my brain kept whirring.

What if Vestalon came back while I was asleep? I had to lock the door. It would be foolish to leave it unlocked even in my neck of the woods. Would I hear him banging on the door?

Knowing Vestalon, if he wanted to reach me, he'd find a way inside, even if it meant scrambling down my chimney like Santa.

I took Milo outside to do his business, and when I was back inside, my boots and coat shucked, I left the outside light on.

He'd need it to find his way back to me.

I woke the next morning after a restless sleep to find my house quiet and empty.

Instead of reheating the breakfast I'd placed in the fridge, I sat at the kitchen counter and ate a bunch of cookies, sobbing into my cocoa. Milo whimpered nearby, and for once my cute doggie couldn't bring me comfort.

What if I never saw Vestalon again? Would he snarl at me if I looked for him in the city?

"So much for the good old calling me in the morning," I told Milo. "I can't believe I fell for an orc playboy who'd use a pretend heat to talk his way into my bed."

Vestalon wouldn't do that, would he?

I didn't think my ex would cheat and look at how that turned out.

My first sigh bled into another. And another.

"I'll give him another day," I said firmly.

But he didn't come back to me the next day either. As I put the last of the cookies into a plastic bag and tossed them into the freezer, I chided myself for believing true love could find me.

"You're strong," I said as I cleared the walk of snow drifted in by the wind.

"You've survived bad shit before and you'll live through this too," I said as I walked down to the end of the drive to examine my oak tree that had no more answers than Milo.

"IF HE WANTS to be with me, he knows where to find me."

But I'd begun to accept I'd never see or hear from Vestalon again.

CHAPTER 16
VESTALON

I'd barely made it to town with the tow truck when my phone rang.

"Yep."

"Oh, Vestalon." It was Grannie. "You've got to help me."

I leaned forward, bracing my palm on the dashboard. "What's wrong?"

"I slipped on the snow. Let me tell you, we didn't have snow in the orc kingdom. It's cold and wet and slippery. My feet went right out from underneath me, and I fell hard."

"Are you alright?"

"Well, that's the thing." She groaned. "Sorry, shifting on the bed."

"Bed?"

"I'm in the hospital. I broke my hip. Thankfully, there's an orthopedic surgeon who knows how to take care of orcs. They're going to put a pin in it tomorrow. A pin, I tell you. I tried to tell him a pin would not be strong enough to secure orc bones, but he insists the pin will hold everything in place. They say I'll be out of the hospital in no time. Walking, would you believe! With a silly little pin in my hip."

I sagged against the seat. "Where are you?"

"I told you, Vesty. I'm in the hospital."

"Which one?"

The tow truck pulled up to the garage, the driver backing the vehicle up and putting it in park. He looked at me, but I waved him away. With a sigh, he got out of the vehicle and started unloading my truck.

"Well, they took me to Settler's Cove General, but it's a small place and the poor ER doctor's eyes widened when she saw them bringing in an orc. Really. You'd think they'd at least have seen us on TV. I was barely there for more than an X-ray before they whisked me back into the ambulance and drove me what feels like halfway across the country."

"Where are you? I'll come to you as soon as I can."

"Aw, that's sweet of you, Vesty, but I'm fine. I do need you to do a little favor for me, however."

"Anything." I adored my grandmother. There wasn't anything she could ask me that I wouldn't do.

"Run my pizza place over the holidays."

"Wait. What? I don't know how to make pizza."

"It's easy. Flour, water, yeast. Mix it around, top it with whatever the customer wants, and bake it."

"You have staff, correct?"

"Yes, I do, and they're able to take direction well.

That's where you come in. I need you to go to my pizza shop and supervise. It's the holidays, the busiest time of the year for humans. I can't afford to close my business."

"My truck went off the road."

"When? Now?"

"After I left you a few days ago."

"Are you hurt?"

"No. I . . . stayed with a wonderful woman during the storm."

"Tell you what. Bring her a pizza as thanks."

I wanted to bring her more than a pizza. "She's my true mate."

"Wonderful, Vesty! About time. Still bring her a pizza."

"I don't know if she likes pizza," I said.

The tow truck driver sat in his seat, staring at me with a lifted unibrow. A glance behind showed me my truck had been removed from the back and placed in front of the shop—one with a closed sign on the window.

"My truck's out of commission," I told my grandmother.

"Take an Uber to my pizza place. I hate to impose at a time like this. You're . . . not in heat, are you?"

"I'm not going to discuss this with you, Grannie."

"You're the one who brought it up."

The driver nudged a clipboard with a bill on it my way. I handed it back with my card, and he ran it through his phone before waving for me to get out of the truck.

"Hold on, Grannie." I covered the phone. "Is there any way I can rent a vehicle or get a ride to the city?"

The guy scratched his head, frowning. "My nephew might be willing to take you for the right price."

That's what I figured.

"It's a deal," I said. I returned to my conversation with my grandmother. "I should be there soon." I'd send Emma another text. Hopefully, she'd understand why I might not be able to spend the holidays with her after all.

"Good," Grannie said. "I'll fill you in on exactly what I need when you get there."

CHAPTER 17

EMMA

By day four, Christmas Eve, I'd given up on Vestalon. I hadn't stopped crying, but I'd realized he'd turned his "fated mate" spiel into a one-night stand.

Sadly, I didn't even merit a two-night stand.

It hurt that he'd do this to me, and it was going to make my chest ache for a very long time. Funny how things get put into perspective when you take time to think. I was upset with my ex when I discovered he'd been cheating. I thought that was the worst thing that could happen to me.

I was wrong.

What my ex did to me was paltry when compared to a guy telling me I was his fated mate to get me into the sack then taking off without even a goodbye in the morning.

"He sucks," I told Milo as I flipped through the channels on the TV. Usually, I'd be all over Frosty or the

Grinch by now. I turned the TV to a channel that played only holiday tunes and stared into the flames flickering in my fireplace. My latest cup of cocoa sat on the coffee table getting cold. I didn't have the heart to take a sip. How could I when it only made me think of Vestalon?

"He really sucks," I announced to the room.

Milo sighed, something crackling beneath his front paws. I thought of seeing what he'd gotten into, but the trash was behind my pantry door, and I didn't have a litter box for him to go foraging. It was probably nothing.

Outside, snow fell lightly. I didn't expect much. No one would slide off the road and crash into my poor tree tonight.

While a woman on the TV crooned about being home for Christmas, tears started trickling down my cheeks. My home was cheery and festive, and I hated that I couldn't sit here and smile at my pretty decorations like I had a few days ago. Savor a funny show. Or sing along with my TV.

Nope, look at me, sobbing for a guy who'd probably forgotten I existed.

I should go to bed. Forget about him. Look forward to the cinnamon rolls I'd made that were slowly rising in the fridge.

Milo hopped off the sofa and trotted to the front door. He scratched it and whined.

"Outside, little buddy?" I asked sadly. I was happy enough to take him out. But there'd be no sliding down the drive and into the arms of a gorgeous orc who'd tell me he loved me.

"I'm such a sappy fool. I fell for his charms, his promises, and the dreams he fed me of a future together. I need to be thankful for what I have, not what I don't. I'm sitting snugly in my cute little house on Christmas Eve. My stocking's hung by the chimney with care, and cookies and milk wait on the mantle for Santa. I don't need an orc's love to make me feel complete."

Rising, I scuffed over to the front door in my kitten slippers. I wore matching jammies, and while I hadn't pulled up the hood with the cute little ears, my long tail swished across the floor behind me.

I stuffed my arms into my coat sleeves and my feet into my boots. Wearing my mittens and with Milo clipped to his leash, I opened the door, determined to brave the latest storm.

A calm silence greeted me as well as a few stars twinkling above.

"Ah," I whispered. "So pretty." I peered around. "Oh, we got more snow than expected." At least six inches, though it had stopped. My neighbor would probably come by the day after tomorrow to clean up my drive if I hadn't blown it out by then. Tomorrow was Christmas. I wasn't sure I'd bother to do anything about it until the next day. Everything looked like it was coated with confectionary sugar.

Whenever it snowed, the world felt renewed, perfect once more.

Sadly, unlike my life. If only a little snow could take care of something like that.

Milo floundered through the drifts, tugging me along the walk. Not again.

"We're not going for a sleigh ride, buddy." I slid after him, hoping I'd stop him before he hit the driveway.

Instead of heading down hill, he took a left, sniffing the snow and snorting.

"You're having fun, aren't you?" I said, okay with hanging out a bit. I'd dressed warmly, and I wanted him to find joy in life too.

He lifted his head and looked my way, his face coated in white. A little woof erupted from his mouth, though it sounded muffled due to the snow.

"We should go inside." I was starting to shiver. While my upper body was warm, my legs were covered with nothing but fleece PJs.

"I don't suppose you've got room for someone to sleep on your couch," someone said from behind me.

I knew that voice. It was etched into my heart.

"Vestalon," I said, not turning.

"I'm finally back."

"Finally?" How could he sound like he'd stepped out for a walk and returned? "You took off. You didn't leave a note. You didn't call or even send me a text."

"But . . . Ah, Milo," he said. "You let me down, buddy."

"Don't blame my dog for something like this." I whirled around, and my breath caught. He looked amazing dressed in jeans and a thick jacket. He even wore a Santa hat on his head.

"Look what Milo's got," Vestalon said. "Frankly, I'm

surprised he hasn't delivered it already." He shook his finger at Milo. "Really, dude, I thought we had a deal."

"Milo has—" My pup nudged my leg with his nose and in his mouth, he held . . . "Paper?"

"A note from me," Vestalon said. "When I went down to the road, the plow truck was passing. He arranged for a tow but before I left, I sent you a text and went back to your house, leaving a note. I put it underneath your cocoa cup in the living room."

"It wasn't there." My voice came out strangled. I wasn't sure what to believe. It was all I could do not to let hope bloom in my heart.

"Would you read the note?"

I took it from Milo, and it looked incredibly worn and somewhat spitty, as if he'd been carrying it around for days.

Maybe he had. How had I missed it?

Emma,

I'm running into town with the plow guy, and I'll find someone to bring me back.

Miss you already. Can't wait to make cookies with you. Are you sure I can't talk you into doing something interesting with a cup of cocoa?

Love,

Vestalon

"You left me a note," I said, my soul melting for him already.

"I texted you a bunch of times too."

"I didn't get them."

He recited a number—except the last two digits were

in the wrong order. "You never texted back, but I had to see you. I had to tell you that I love you, that I want to spend my life with you."

"Vestalon," I breathed. "I must've typed my number in wrong because I didn't get even one message."

He strode right up to me. "Can we make up for lost time?"

"You said something about sleeping on my couch."

"Well, actually, I was hoping to find my way back into your bed."

When he held out his arms, I jumped into them.

And when he kissed me, Milo barked.

In the sound, I heard doggy approval.

CHAPTER 18
EMMA
EPILOGUE

Six Month Later

"**W**ife. Mate," Vestalon growled.

"You may now kiss the bride," Kassia said. She'd filled out the paperwork to get her license to perform marriages and ours was her first.

We got married behind my cute house. Vestalon moved in with me, saying he loved the country life, and he was ready to slow down. He'd still go into the city once a week, but he'd hired managers and would handle the rest from the office we'd set up in one of the two rooms we'd built onto our house.

As for me, I still had my job at the library, and I adored it.

Vestalon lifted me up, and his mouth captured mine, just like he'd captured my heart months ago when he crashed into my tree. While I wanted to wrap my legs around him and stroke his horns, I resisted.

Later.

"Congratulations, you two," Thraal called out with humor brightening his voice.

We broke apart, gazing at each other. So much love filled his eyes. I could stare into them forever.

Autumn, Thraal's wife, skipped over to hug him. He leaned to the side to kiss her cheek before grinning my way.

Jarum joined Kassia, kissing her and stroking her baby bump. She was only four months along but showing already.

Rexin and Adeline had also come to our wedding. We'd met them when we visited Thraal. They owned the amusement park one town over and had gotten married not long ago. We planned to hit the park soon and ride the elephant carriage ride.

Rexin and Adeline stood with the rest of our guests, Rexin's tall son between them. Even my best friend, Lexi, had come from my old hometown. I might try to fix her up with Cruger, Rexin's brother, while she was in town.

As I slid down Vestalon's body, people and orcs cheered and shouted congrats.

Grinning and holding hands, we walked down the aisle between our friends with Milo—dressed in a big red bow—yipping with happiness beside us.

Jarum's brother, a hot-shot goalie for an orc sports team, had also come to the wedding. I heard he'd created a scandal. Something about doing something orc-like that unintentionally insulted a reporter. Jarum had stepped in to be his unofficial PR person and was exploring options to improve his brother's rep.

A big tent had been set up beside my house, where we'd hold our reception. We were serving a mix of human and orc dishes, combining our two cultures just like we were combining us.

Later tonight, after we'd celebrated our marriage in our own special way, I had a surprise for my mate. His heat had worked its way through while we were apart, and I imagined that was tough, but we'd spent a lot of time making up for the loss.

I couldn't wait to let him know that our first child would be born around Christmas. What better time of the year than that?

"Does this mean you now have someone to snow blow your drive?" my neighbor called out with a laugh as we passed.

"I believe she does," Vestalon said. He looked my way. "What do you say, love? Do you need him to plow your drive, or do you think I can handle it for you?"

My smile made my cheeks ache. "If there's any plowing that's going to be done, love, you'll be the one to do it."

I hope you enjoyed Vestalon & Emma's story!
Next is Gaming the Orc,
then Orc-wardly Yours, the final
book in the Love at First Orc Series!

Check out the first chapter of Gaming the Orc . . .

GAMING THE ORC

My popping-out-of-cake days are numbered when I fall into the lap of a brawny orc, and he claims me as his bride.

As a favor to an orc friend, I agree to fake date his sports star brother to improve his image.

I'm not supposed to pop out of a big cake at a bachelor party. Or give a gorgeous orc a lap dance.

As for getting locked in the elevator with him and continuing that dance?

Not supposed to do that either.

Turns out the hot-shot orc sports god, Brogis, is my one-night stand. Or should I call him my one-elevator stand? Same difference, right?

The press loves the idea that he's dating a kindergarten teacher. And while I'm not so thrilled that they chase me for the inside scoop, it's nice to reconnect with my elevator crush. To hide from the press, I move in with Brogis. Somewhere between cheering for his team and sampling his favorite orc dish at a diner, I fall in love. But with his image improving, our fake relationship's heading for a quick breakup.

Unless I can convince Brogis to make this real . . .

Gaming the Orc is Book 4 in the Love At First Orc Series.

Expect heated encounters with a gorgeous orc who's creative with his . . . (cough), size difference, he falls first but keeps it hidden, touch her and I'll unalive you, trapped together in an elevator, instalove, a curvy woman, and fated mates in heat. HEA guaranteed.

Love at First Orc Series

Orc Charming

Orc-us Pocus

Orc-ishly Ever After

Tinsel & Tusks

Gaming the Orc

Orc-wardly Yours

Companion Stories

Single Orc Dad

CHAPTER 1
FLORA

"I am not wearing that red thing and popping out of the cake," I shouted to my friend, Ginny. "I'm impulsive but even I have my limits."

"I know the cake's silly, but guys love this sort of thing," she said. "Pretty please? This job means a lot to me."

As an event planner, this bachelor party was her first big gig.

I was sitting at home reading a good book when she called, begging me to help her out of a bind. I thought she'd had one too many and needed a ride home. Or that her blind date turned out to be a jerk.

Not that she wanted me to wear almost no clothing and pop out of a cake at the bachelor party she'd organized.

Now we stood inside what felt like a closet adjacent to the room where the bachelor party was in full force, if the shouts and barks of laughter from human and male orcs were anything to go by.

A few years ago, orcs emerged from a previously unknown city deep within a big mountain range in the middle of the country. They formed a treaty with humans and joined our society, taking jobs and dating. My cousin, Kassia, had recently married her orc husband, Jarum.

Jarum had recently asked me to do a favor for him, and I'd agreed. Date his hot-shot sports god brother for a week or so to improve the guy's rep? Count me in.

But that was next week. Cake-popping was on the agenda for now.

I glared at Ginny, wondering how in the world I could get out of this. "Why didn't you tell me what you needed me to do when you called in your favor?"

She smirked. "Would you have agreed if I'd told you?"

"I can't believe you still think I owe you."

"Did I or did I not slip Jimmy the note you wrote him in ninth grade?"

"That was eleven years ago. I barely remember him."

"Just as well. He's got a dad bod and ten kids to prove it."

"Ten?" I shuddered. I like kids and all, but one or two will be enough for me.

Good thing he'd politely told her he wasn't interested after reading my note.

She nudged the red slinky outfit my way again. "Please? The real cake-popping woman is sick. We couldn't have her throwing up all over the bachelor party, now could we?"

"Look at it." I plucked the red number from her fingers and lifted it, shaking my head. "The bottom half's a thong. It might as well be crotchless."

"So keep your legs together."

"Who wears something like this anyway?"

She grinned. "I would."

I thrust it toward her. "Then you jump out of the cake."

"Orcs can be jealous when their fated mate flaunts her body in front of other guys."

"Your fiancé's not hurting you, is he?" I snarled, ready to rip off an orc's head. Try to, anyway.

"Not in the least. He's a sweetie." Her sappy smile fell. "But I'm organizing the event, and I'm needed in the kitchen. Do this for me, please? I'll never ask for anything else again."

I adored Ginny. Truly. But how in the world would I get the guts to do something like this? "It'll barely cover my boobs. In case you haven't noticed, I'm a D-cup. And plus sized. I'm going to bulge in all the wrong places."

"All you have to do is pop out, shout surprise, flirt a little, then leave. You'll never see any of them again. No one will know it's you."

I scrunched shoulders. "Alright. But you owe *me* a favor now."

"Yay." Ginny hugged me. "Thanks. You're a lifesaver."

"We're talking about me in a red slinky number popping out of a cake, not doing CPR."

"It'll be fun. We'll laugh about it later."

"If you say so." With a growl, I lifted my dress up and over my head and handed it to her.

A frown filled her pretty face. With her white-blonde hair and big blue eyes, she was gorgeous. Although, my cousin Kassia often said my auburn hair and blue eyes made me striking.

"Remove your undies too," Ginny said. "They'll stick out the sides of the thong."

"Yeah, yeah." Turning away, I unclipped my bra and shimmied out of them and my panties, tucking both into my dress pocket. I tugged the one-piece of red scraps of silky material up over my hips and stuffed my arms through the spaghetti straps, wiggling them onto my shoulders. After shifting the triangles to cover my nipples and wrenching the thong bottom into place between my butt cheeks, I pivoted back to face her.

"You look amazing," Ginny breathed.

Looking down, I winced. "I'm too . . . lush."

"You're perfect." She tugged on the lacy string snaking across my belly to connect the outfit, moving it to the middle of my belly. "Shoes." She pointed to a gaudy pair lying on the floor.

"They've got five inches heels. I won't be able to stand, let alone walk in them, and you expect me to gyrate around the room, flirting?"

"Sway your hips. Tease your fingers across a few guys' jawlines. They won't be able to look past your boobs to note your heels."

So she says. She'd be in the kitchen while I'd be playing porn star.

"Tonight could be your chance, you know, to let loose and have fun. You've told me a bunch of times that you don't get out enough."

"I was thinking dating. The movies or dinner. Not being the highlight of a bunch of drunk guys' evening."

"Tonight, you're not Flora Brennen. You're Pussy Luscious, the sexy woman every single one of those guys will fantasize about later. Well, other than the groom. He's taken."

As if. "Pussy Luscious? Who comes up with names like that?"

She grinned. "Someone who jumps out of a cake. Roll with it. *Be* Pussy." She undid my hair from the loose bun I kept it in all the time, fluffing the long strands until they puffed around my shoulders and face. "I can't imagine why you wear this gorgeous hair up."

"It gets in my way." It was hard to be taken seriously with my curvy body, Ariel hair, and baby blue eyes.

Ginny glanced at her phone. "Into the cake with you, my dear. It's nearly time."

Ugh, ugh, ugh. Tottering in the heels, I stepped onto the chair beside the enormous pink monstrosity and clambered up and over the side. Straightening, I had to yank a triangle back over my right nipple that had popped into view.

If anyone found out I'd done this, I was never going to live it down.

Ginny lifted the top and approached me. "Sit on the

stool. Remember, the hotel guy will wheel you out. Music will play and end in a crescendo. Push off the top and pop out with your arms lifted and a big smile on your face. While everyone cheers—"

"Ogles my bod."

She rolled her eyes. "Just sashay around the room, shaking your hips. Flirt if you want. Hell, do a tease for them if you feel inspired. Then scoot back here and morph back to Flora the kindergarten teacher again, leaving Pussy the cake-popping goddess behind." She dropped the cake top above me, leaving me in muted darkness. "Get ready!"

The door opened and closed. She opened the door, and the staffer stepped inside.

A guy grumbled. "One cake coming up." His voice lifted. "Hold on in there. It's showtime."

The cake started moving. Shouts erupted, followed by slinky music. The cake came to a stop, and the music grew louder, ending in a final bang and silence broken only by hoots of laughter.

"Gentlemen and gentleorcs?" someone called out. "I present to you . . . Pussy Luscious!"

I braced the cake top and straightened, thrusting it to the side. "Ta da!"

Everyone cheered. A tune worthy of a strip club erupted overhead as I climbed out of the cake and onto the floor, holding my arms out to keep from falling on the stupid heels.

The guys' gazes ate me up, so to speak. Focused on my scantily clad body, not one of them looked at my face.

I swayed my hips and sashayed in a circle to the shouts of orcs and guys alike. Loosening up, I burst through my lingering inhibitions. Ginny was right. Tonight, I could be whoever I pleased.

I *became* Pussy.

As Ginny had suggested, I trailed a fingertip along one chiseled orc jawline after another until I reached the incredibly hot guy sitting at the end of the line.

Stopped in front of him, I wasn't sure where my bravery came from, but I leaned toward him, bracing my hand on his muscular chest. While the other guys shouted and cheered, pretended to hump the orc's tree-trunk thigh. Hopefully, this wasn't the one getting married. No, the guy to the left wore a shirt emblazoned with *Groom*.

While everyone around us hooted and clapped, I locked eyes with this gorgeous orc, trailing my fingertips across his chest and along his sinfully delicious forearms.

His grin was infectious. I'd never been this attracted to someone in my life.

It didn't take any urging on his part for me to clamber up into his lap, my legs straddling his hips.

As the music played, I gyrated in his lap.

Love at First Orc Series

ABOUT THE AUTHOR

Ava Ross is a two-time *USA Today* Bestselling author who has written numerous titles, all of them featuring sweet and steamy romance. She fell for men with unusual features when she first watched Star Wars, where alien creatures have gone mainstream. She lives in New England with her husband (who is sadly not an alien, though he is still cute in his own way), her kids, and a few assorted pets.

SERIES BY AVA

Mail-Order Brides of Crakair
Brides of Driegon
Fated Mates of the Ferlaern Warriors
Fated Mates of the Xilan Warriors
Holiday with a Cu'zod Warrior
Galaxy Games
Alien Warrior Abandoned/
Shattered Galaxies
Beastly Alien Boss
Bride of the Fae
A Sci-Fi Holiday Tail
Monsterville, USA
Monster on Board
(co-written with Alana Khan)
A Monster Worth Fighting For
(Monster Between the Sheets)
Love at First Orc
Monster Mate Hunt

Single Titles
Dad Bod Dragon
Mated to the Dragon
Jasmine's Enchanted Genie
Swamp Thing (You Make My Heart Sing)

You can find my books on Amazon.

www.ingramcontent.com/pod-product-compliance
Lightning Source LLC
Chambersburg PA
CBHW021013160726
47994CB00006B/2494